STORIES FROM ANCIENT EGYPT

by

**Joyce
Tyldesley**

Illustrated by

**Julian
Heath**

First published in Great Britain in 2005
Rutherford Press Limited, 37 Rutherford Drive, Bolton, BL5 1DJ
Registered Office: 52 Chorley New Road, Bolton, BL1 4AP

www.rutherfordpress.co.uk

A CIP catalogue record of this book is available from the British Library

ISBN 978-0-9547622-1-6

Printed in Great Britain by the MPG Books Group, Bodmin and King's Lynn

CONTENTS

THIS BOOK BELONGS TO:

This large oval ring is called a **cartouche**. Egyptian kings used to write their names in cartouches, and you can too, using the hieroglyphic signs below.

A	𓄿	**J**	𓆓	**S**	—⚬— or ❘		
B	𓃀	**K**	𓎡	**T**	⌂		
C	use K	**L**	𓃭	**U**	use W		
D	⬯	**M**	𓅓	**V**	use F		
E	use I	**N**	〰	**W**	𓅱		
F	𓆑	**O**	use W	**X**	use K+S		
G	𓎼	**P**	☐	**Y**	𓏭		
H	𓎛	**Q**	use K+W	**Z**	use S		
I	𓇋	**R**	⬭				

ABOUT THIS BOOK

When I was a schoolgirl (a very long time ago!) I loved reading the myths and legends of ancient Greece and Rome. I would have loved to read the stories of ancient Egypt too, but I could not find them in the bookshops.

In this book I have collected together some of the most popular ancient Egyptian stories. One of them, the Battle of Kadesh, tells the true story of Ramesses the Great and his fight against the Hittite enemies of Egypt. The rest of the stories are fiction - made up stories.

Some of these are stories that the Egyptians told to explain the things that puzzled them - how did the world start? Who ruled Egypt at the beginning of time? But most are stories that were told as pure entertainment.

Happy reading!

Joyce Tyldesley

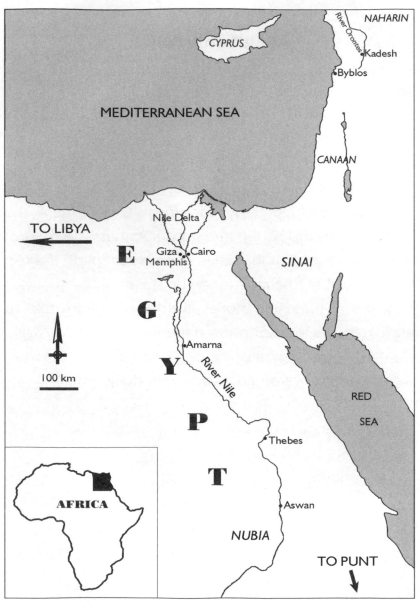

NAHARIN

River Orontes

•Kadesh

CYPRUS

•Byblos

MEDITERRANEAN SEA

CANAAN

Nile Delta

TO LIBYA

E

SINAI

Giza •Cairo
Memphis

G

100 km

Y

Amarna

River Nile

P

RED

SEA

Thebes

T

AFRICA

Aswan

NUBIA

TO PUNT

6

ABOUT EGYPT

As you can see from the map opposite, Egypt is a long thin country in the northeast (top right) corner of Africa. The River Nile is a wide, deep river that flows northwards along a valley that runs through the middle of Egypt. The river divides in the north to form a flat, triangular region called the Nile Delta. To either side of the Nile valley there are fertile fields, then dry deserts, and finally steep mountains.

To the south of Egypt is the land of Nubia (modern Sudan). To the north is the Mediterranean Sea. To the west, over the desert and the mountains, is Libya, and to the east, again over the desert and the mountains, is the Red Sea. There is only one easy way to walk out of Egypt. In the northeast corner the Sinai desert forms a natural bridge that allows people to travel overland to the ancient land of Canaan (modern Israel).

Many thousands of years ago people started to live alongside the River Nile. They used the river in many different ways. Nile water was used for cooking, washing and laundry. The Nile became a highway for boats and a drain for sewage. The mud along the riverbank made an excellent building material - in Ancient Egypt all the houses and palaces were made from sun-baked mud bricks. And the fish in the Nile were a free source of healthy food.

Most important of all, the Nile allowed the farmers to grow their crops. Every year, from July to October, the Nile swelled and burst her banks. You might think that this was a bad thing, but the Egyptians welcomed the floodwaters because they made the fields wet. As Egypt is a hot African country with little rain, the crops would not grow without this water. Soon the fields were completely covered. The towns and cities, which were always built on high ground, became little islands linked by raised paths. The waters shrank back in late October leaving the wet fields ready for planting. The farmers sowed their crops and waited. In late spring they gathered a wonderful harvest of grain, fruits and vegetables. The land then had time to dry out under the hot sun, before the river flooded again in July.

ABOUT HIEROGLYPHS

The first Egyptian scribes used hieroglyphs; writing made up of hundreds of different drawings. Hieroglyphs could be read from either left to right or right to left; scribes could choose whichever way they fancied!

Hieroglyphic writing was beautiful to look at. But it took a long time to write. So a new and faster type of writing was invented. Hieratic writing is a joined up form of hieroglyphs. It is always read from right to left. Most of the stories in this book were written in hieratic. Only the story of the Battle of Kadesh, a true story, was carved in old-fashioned hieroglyphs on Egypt's temple walls.

The scribes used reed paint-brushes dipped in coloured ink. They did not have paper. Sometimes they wrote on broken pottery or flakes of stone. These types of writings are called ostraca. But more often they wrote on papyrus scrolls. Papyrus was a tall plant that grew in the Egyptian marshes. The Egyptians soon learned that thin strips of papyrus, laid side by side and flattened with a mallet, made an excellent form of paper.

1

THE CREATION OF THE WORLD

In the beginning nothing existed but the swirling sea. There was no land and there was no sky. No gods, no people, no light and no time. Only water. But deep within the dark sea a small egg was floating. Hidden in that egg was a spark of life which struggled to escape.

Suddenly the egg cracked open. Life had started. With a huge roar, and a great surge of water, an island rose out of chaos. And sitting on the island was the god Atum. Atum shone like the sun and brought light to his new land. But there was no one else on his island, and he felt very lonely.

Atum decided to make some more gods. He spat and he sneezed, and spit flew out of his mouth and snot shot out of his nose and splattered on the ground. Yuk! But two beautiful children grew from this nasty mess. Atum named his son Shu and his daughter Tefnut. Shu became the god of the air, and Tefnut became the goddess of moisture. And Atum, Shu and Tefnut lived safe from harm on their island in the middle of the sea.

Atum loved his children dearly, but he worried about them all the time. He never let them out of his sight because he was certain that something bad would happen to them. One dreadful day he looked away, just for a second. That was long enough. Shu and Tefnut wandered away from their father and fell into the sea.

Atum saw them struggling as they vanished under the waves. His eyes filled with tears and everything was blurred; he could hardly see. He searched the depths of the sea until he found the twins and carried them back to the island. With Shu and Tefnut safe on dry land, Atum's tears of sorrow turned to tears of joy. The tears fell onto the island, and from them grew men and women.

Tefnut gave birth to twins. Geb was the handsome god of the earth. He lay down and carried the green fields, the damp marshes and the great River Nile on his back. His laughter brought earthquakes and his anger brought famine.

Nut was the beautiful goddess of the sky. She stretched herself above the earth with her fingers and toes resting on the horizons of the north, east, south and west. Her laughter brought thunder, and her tears brought rain. Along her deep blue body the stars and moon twinkled and shone at night.

ABOUT THE CREATION OF THE WORLD

Some Egyptians believed that the world began when a beetle crawled out of the petals of a beautiful flower. Others thought that the world hatched from an egg laid by a gigantic goose! The tale of Atum and his island was the creation story told by the priests who worshipped the sun god, Re.

Egypt had hundreds of gods and goddesses. Some looked like ordinary people, some looked like animals, and some were a weird mixture of animal heads stuck on human bodies. Many of the gods and goddesses had several different disguises. Atum was one of these. He usually looked like a man wearing the crown of Egypt, but he could also be a snake or a beetle.

The Egyptians lived on the edge of a desert; they knew that water was necessary for life. This story would have reminded them of what happened every year when their own fields re-appeared from under the Nile floodwaters.

WHAT DO YOU THINK?

1. Why was the River Nile important to the Egyptians?

2. Why did the Egyptians not need roads?

3. What sort of foods do you think the Egyptians ate?

14

2

HATHOR AND THE RED BEER

A long time ago gods, goddesses and people lived together in Egypt. They were ruled by Re, the sun god. Re had been king of Egypt for many, many years. He had ruled wisely and well. The fields were golden with ripe corn, the river was full of tasty fish, and the yellow deserts glittered with flecks of gold. But not everyone was happy. Some of the people thought that Re was far too old to be king, and they started to plot against him.

King Re saw what was happening and grew angry and upset. He called a secret meeting. That night all the gods and goddesses came tiptoeing into Re's splendid palace. They crept into the great hall, and stood in silence on either side of Re's golden throne.

Politely, the gods and goddesses bowed to greet their king. Then Re spoke.

"Some of the people are plotting against me. They are hiding in the desert, making secret plans. They think that I can't see them, but they are very stupid. I am a god, so I can see everything! I think that it would be a good idea if

15

I killed all the people, good and bad. Do you agree that this is the best thing for me to do?"

The gods did agree. All the men and women must die. That would put an end to their plotting, for sure.

Hathor, the gentle daughter of King Re, was told to kill all the people of Egypt. She transformed into Sekhmet, the fierce lion-headed goddess of destruction. Then, with a mighty roar, she set to work. Soon the desert ran red with blood as she hunted down the people and killed many of them, one by one. Tired, but happy with her work, she stopped for the day. She licked her red lips, transformed back into Hathor, and returned home.

Re welcomed his daughter back with a hug, but he was worried. He had not liked watching Hathor kill the people; in fact watching her had made him feel quite ill. He had decided that there should be no more deaths. But how was he going to stop Hathor? She had grown to like the taste of human blood.

Re devised a clever plan. Sending for his swiftest messengers he ordered them to bring vast quantities of red paint. At the same time dozens of serving maids set to work grinding hundreds of baskets of grain. The grain was used to brew seven thousand jars of beer. Then the paint was stirred into the beer, turning it blood red.

The next day was the day that Hathor planned to destroy the rest of the people. King Re got up early. He travelled to the fields and poured out the seven thousand jars of beer so that the land was flooded with red liquid. Hathor saw the foaming red beer and thought that it was blood. Suddenly she felt very thirsty. She bent down and drank the beer - all seven thousand jars! Then she hiccuped, and grew sleepy. She lay down in the fields and took a long nap. That evening Hathor returned home happy. She did not realise that she had failed to kill all the men and women of Egypt.

ABOUT HATHOR AND THE RED BEER

Re the sun god was one of Egypt's most important gods. He was worshipped throughout the land, but his great temple was in the north near the city of Memphis. The Egyptian artists usually showed Re as a falcon (a fierce bird of prey). But sometimes they showed him as a man with a falcon head, and occasionally he was a circular sun with wings.

Re's daughter Hathor could look like a woman or a cow. Hathor was a beautiful, gentle girl, but when she grew angry she became dangerous - she transformed into Sekhmet, a lion-headed goddess who breathed fire.

Hathor liked to drink beer. She was not the only one. Beer was Egypt's most popular drink and men, women, and children drank it at every meal! The beer was a thick, sweet, soup-like drink with so many chewy bits some Egyptians drank it through a straw to avoid swallowing the chunks.

For a long time Egyptologists thought that Egyptian beer was made by crumbling bread into warm water - yuk! But modern experiments have shown that this is not true. We now think that the Egyptians made their beer from part-grown barley. Modern brewers use a similar recipe.

WHAT DO YOU THINK?

1. What did the sun god Re look like?

2. Why did the people want to kill Re?

3. How did Re stop Hathor from killing all the people?

4. What did Egyptian beer taste like?

19

3

THE STORY OF ISIS AND OSIRIS

The goddess Nut had two baby boys called Osiris and Seth and two baby girls called Isis and Nephthys. Osiris, Isis and Nephthys were happy, sunny babies who grew up to be good children and fine gods. But Seth was a mean, cross baby who grew into a naughty toddler, a grumpy teenager and an evil god.

Osiris was chosen to be king of Egypt. He was a very good king indeed. He taught the people how to work in the fields and grow crops. His sister Isis was his queen. She taught the women how to weave cloth and bake bread. The people were very happy with their new king and queen.

But there was one person who was not at all happy. Seth was so filled with jealousy he could hardly speak to anyone. He had always wanted to be king of Egypt, and now his brother was king instead! Seth decided that Osiris must die so that he, Seth, could be king in his place. Seth started to plot his brother's murder.

Seth planned a magnificent party. The tables were

piled high with joints of beef and mutton. There were roast birds, grilled fish and heaps of bread and sweet cakes. There were salads, fresh vegetables and mountains of sweet fruit. And to wash it all down there were many jars of wine, and even more jars of beer. The air was perfumed with the scent of many flowers, and musicians sang and played sweet music. Never had there been such a party.

Seth had invited seventy-two of his best friends - all of them evil men - to the party. But the guest of honour was his brother Osiris. The guests ate and drank then ate again until they were full. Then Seth signalled to his servants, and a long, narrow box was dragged into the centre of the room. The box was beautiful. Carved from the finest wood, it was decorated with silver and gold.

Seth spoke. The box was a party game. If any of the guests could fit into the box he could keep it as a prize. There was a scramble as Seth's friends rushed forward. But none of them fitted into the box. Then Osiris took his turn. He was very thin, and was easily able to lie down in the box. It was a perfect fit. But before Osiris could sit up again Seth slammed the lid shut and locked it. Osiris was trapped inside the box - it had become a coffin.

Suddenly the party was over. Acting quickly Seth

covered the coffin in lead then dragged it to the River Nile and threw it in. He laughed as he saw the box float slowly down river and bob out to sea. Now Seth could be king of Egypt. There was no one to stop him. But Seth had forgotten about his brave sister Isis.

Osiris had vanished, but Isis could not forget him. She spent many years wandering along the mighty River Nile, hoping to find news of her brother. At last she heard a rumour that a precious wooden box had been washed ashore in the far away land of Byblos. The box had rested against a young tree, and the tree had grown around the box. The tree had then been cut down, and used as a pillar to hold up the roof of the king's palace.

Isis left Egypt and travelled to Byblos. Arriving at the palace she sat in the garden and cried and cried. She didn't know what to do next - how would she find Osiris? The queen of Byblos's rather scruffy serving maids found Isis and made friends with her. And Isis, happy again, braided their hair and perfumed their skin so that they looked smart and smelt wonderful. When the queen of Byblos saw her maids looking neat and tidy she wished to meet the woman who had styled their hair. So Isis was introduced to the queen of Byblos, and became nursemaid to her baby son.

All day long Isis cared for the baby prince. But at night, when no one could see, she turned herself into a bird and flew round and round the pillar that held Osiris. Isis wept as she flew, and her noisy sobs woke the queen. The queen, seeing her baby lying unattended, demanded to know what was happening. Isis told her the whole sad story, and the queen at once gave her the pillar. Isis cut into the wood, and uncovered the coffin that still held Osiris.

Isis set sail for Egypt where she hid the coffin in the desert. But Seth, out hunting alone in the moonlight, discovered it. Seth could not believe his eyes. He had thought that he had seen the last of Osiris and here he was, back in Egypt again. Filled with rage he opened the coffin, hacked his dead brother into fourteen pieces, and flung the body-bits far and wide.

Transforming themselves into giant birds Isis and Nephthys searched high and low for their brother. After a great deal of hard work they recovered his scattered parts, fitted Osiris back together again, and wrapped him in bandages. Then Isis used her magic to bring Osiris back to life.

The spell worked. Osiris was alive again, but he was a mummy who could no longer live in Egypt. Osiris went to the Underworld where he ruled the Kingdom of the Dead.

ABOUT ISIS AND OSIRIS

Osiris, the dead king of Egypt, was bandaged and brought back to life by his sisters. He had become the first Egyptian mummy! We can recognise Osiris in Egyptian art because he has the stiff, white, bandaged body of a mummy. His head, which is never bandaged, wears a crown to prove that he has once been a king of Egypt. Osiris might look sinister or frightening to us, but the Egyptians loved him. They found the idea that they would live again after mummification very comforting.

Why did the Egyptians mummify their dead? They developed this gruesome habit because they wanted to make sure that their bodies would not turn to skeletons after death. This was important to them, because they believed that the spirit or soul of the dead person used the body as a home.

How did they go about making a mummy? Well, this was a secret process, so we are not entirely sure. It's not exactly something that we can practise at home! But we know that it was very important to remove the soft inner parts of the body, because these are the bits that rot first. The brain was removed through the nose, using a long probe and a long-handled spoon. The guts and lungs were taken out through a slit cut in the side, although the heart was left in place so that the mummy could use it in the afterlife. The body was then covered in a special type of salt - natron salt - and left to dry for forty days. Finally the body was wrapped in many layers of linen bandages until it looked exactly like the dead Osiris.

Mummification was a religious ritual. So, while the undertakers worked, they recited the spells and prayers that would make sure that the mummy was able to come back to life. Tucked inside the bandages there were special charms and jewellery that would also help the mummy to survive. Some of the undertakers even wore special masks while they worked, so that they looked like gods.

WHAT DO YOU THINK?

1. Why did Seth hate his brother Osiris?

2. How did Seth trick his brother?

3. Why did the Egyptians make mummies?

4. Can you guess how much linen cloth was needed to wrap a mummy?

4

THE QUARREL BETWEEN HORUS AND SETH

King Osiris had left the land of the living and now ruled the land of the dead. His baby son, Horus, should have been the next king of Egypt. But Osiris's evil brother Seth had seized the throne. For many years Seth ruled Egypt, and Horus and his mother Isis were forced to hide in the marshes.

Eventually Horus grew up. He left the safety of the marshes to claim his throne. But Seth liked being king - he did not want Horus to take his place. So Horus and Seth asked the council of the gods and goddesses to choose between them. But the gods and goddesses could not make their minds up. Some thought that Horus should be king because he was the son of Osiris. Others thought that Horus was too young to rule Egypt. They thought that Seth should continue to be king because he was a clever and brave god.

The quarrel between Horus and Seth lasted for eighty years. The other gods and goddesses grew very bored. They wanted the matter to be settled, once and for all.

28

But they still could not choose between Horus and Seth. Every council meeting ended with the gods and goddesses hurling insults at each other like rude children in a playground.

"I think Seth should be king."

"But I think Horus should be king."

"No one cares what you think, dimwit. You are an unimportant god."

"Well, I may be unimportant, but at least I am not smelly. Your breath stinks!"

The gods and goddesses decided that they should take a break. Perhaps if they left the stuffy, dark meeting hall and had a picnic in the fresh air, they would be able to reach a decision. So they travelled to an island in the middle of the River Nile and sat down to enjoy a meal in the sunlight. But Isis was left behind and the boatman was given strict instructions not to let her cross the river.

The gods and goddesses had forgotten that Isis had strong magical powers. Transforming into a poor old woman she hobbled up to the boatman and pleaded with him.

"Please take me across to the island, sir. I am just a harmless grandmother who wants to take a bowl of porridge to her grandson. He has been looking after the cattle on the island for five long days without food, and he has grown very hungry."

The boatman was worried. This bent old crone looked nothing like the beautiful Isis, but how could he be sure? When Isis offered her valuable gold ring as payment for the ride he decided to take a chance. The boatman let the goddess board his boat, and she sailed to the island.

Isis spied on the gods and goddesses as they tucked into their picnic. Then Seth looked up. He caught a glimpse of Isis, but he did not recognise her. She had abandoned her disguise, and had become the most beautiful girl in the world. Seth thought that it would be good fun to talk to this gorgeous girl. He left his food and, leaning against a tall sycamore tree, called out in his smoothest voice.

"Hi there beautiful! What's a lovely girl like you doing all alone in a place like this? Let me be your friend and we can walk and talk together holding hands in the cool shade of the green trees."

Isis replied in a soft whisper, telling a sad tale:

"First let me tell you my story, stranger. Once I was the wife of a herdsman. We were a happy family, my husband, our son and I. Then my husband died, and my young son began to look after our cattle. But a stranger came and seized our cattle. The stranger threatened to beat my son and throw him out of our home. What do you think of my story, stranger?"

Seth, who was nowhere near as clever as he thought he was, failed to spot the trap. Without thinking, his eyes filling with tears, he spoke.

"My poor, beautiful girl. What a terrible story. Your son has been cheated. The stranger should be beaten and thrown off your land. Your son should have his dead father's job."

Hearing Seth's words Isis transformed into a giant black bird. She flew to perch in the topmost branches of the sycamore tree and shrieked down at Seth.

"You agree that a son should always have his dead father's job. You have been judged by your own words."

Realising that he had been tricked, Seth burst into tears. He ran back to the picnic, and told the other gods and goddesses what had happened. Then he challenged Horus to a duel. They would each transform into a hippopotamus and dive to the depths of the sea. They would stay underwater for three whole months. The one that stayed under the water longest would be king of Egypt. Horus agreed. Taking a deep breath the two hippopotami plunged side by side into the sea.

Isis sat on the shore and cried. She was so worried that Seth would kill her son that she decided to help Horus win the contest. She took a very long piece of flax and twisted it into a rope. Next she fetched a lump of copper, melted it, and cast it in the form of a harpoon. She tied the rope to the harpoon, and threw it into the water.

Under the water the harpoon speared Horus's leg. He gave a loud shriek.

"Help me mother, tell your harpoon to let me go. It has speared your son, Horus."

Isis ordered her magic harpoon to release Horus, and threw it into the water again. This time it was Seth's turn to wail.

"Isis, my sister, don't harm me. I have never done anything to hurt you, but you seem to hate me more than you would hate a complete stranger."

Hearing her brother's words, and quite forgetting how Seth had killed her husband Osiris, Isis ordered her harpoon to release Seth. The two hippopotami came up from the water and their quarrel continued.

Seth issued another challenge to Horus. They would each build a stone boat and have a race. The winner would be king of Egypt. Horus decided to cheat! He built a wooden boat, then covered it in plaster and painted it grey so that it looked like a ship carved from solid stone. When the race started, Seth's stone boat sank at once. Of course Horus's wooden boat floated and he won the race easily.

Realising that he had been tricked, Seth transformed into a hippopotamus and dived under the water to make a hole in the side of Horus's boat. The angry Horus seized a copper harpoon and threw it into the water to spear Seth and kill him. The gods and goddesses, who had gathered to watch the race of the stone boats, had to drag the furious Horus away from his uncle.

Eventually the gods and goddesses had a brainwave. They would write to Osiris, and ask for his advice. To no one's great surprise the answer came back:

"My son Horus should be king of Egypt, of course."

The gods and goddesses had finally made up their minds. Horus son of Osiris was crowned, and placed on the throne of his father Osiris. As for Seth, he was not punished but sent to live in the sky with the sun god Re.

ABOUT HORUS AND SETH

Seth is a strange god. He looks weird - a mixture of an aardvark and a long-eared pig or donkey - and his behaviour is very odd. Seth lies, cheats and even kills his brother to become king of Egypt. This is not really the sort of thing that we would expect from a god, but the Egyptians had no problems with Seth's bad behaviour. They believed that their gods and goddesses were not always good and wise; they could be rude or thoughtless and some, like Seth, could be downright bad. But Seth manages to come good in the end. In his new job, he protects the sun god Re against his enemies.

Horus, son of Osiris and Isis, is the hero of the story. He appears in Egyptian art either as a child or as a falcon.

Isis, the mother of Horus, is a beautiful woman with strong magical powers. She is a mistress of disguise, able to become an old woman, a beautiful girl or a bird. Isis is also a healer - she is able to bring the dead and bandaged Osiris back to life. But above all she is a devoted mother who cares for her young son, Horus.

WHAT DO YOU THINK?

1. Why do some gods and goddesses think that Horus should be king of Egypt?

2. Why do the other gods and goddesses think that Seth should be king?

3. Who do you think should be king of Egypt?

4. What does Isis look like?

5

THREE MAGICAL STORIES

King Khufu was a very lucky man. He was the richest king in the world. He had a magnificent palace, a huge pyramid tomb, and great heaps of gold. He should have been very happy indeed. But night had fallen, and Khufu was bored. He couldn't go outside to hunt or fish because it was too dark. He didn't want to play a game, and he felt too tired to read. So he sent for his family, and asked them to tell him stories. These are three of the stories that the royal princes told their father in the palace that night.

THE WAX CROCODILE:
THE STORY TOLD BY PRINCE KHAEFRE

Once upon a time there was a priest called Webaoner. Webaoner was a happily married man who owned a large house in the country with a green garden, shady fruit trees and a calm blue pool. By the side of the pool was a gazebo where Webaoner and his wife would sit

37

and eat their meals, enjoying the peace and beauty of their garden.

But one day a terrible thing happened. Webaoner's beautiful young wife fell in love with another man. She sent her new boyfriend expensive presents, and arranged to meet him in secret in the gazebo next to the pool. Being a silly young woman, she asked the family servant to clean the gazebo first, so that it would be tidy when her guest arrived. Of course the loyal servant told his master exactly what was happening in his garden.

Webaoner was extremely upset by his wife's behaviour. He said nothing, but plotted his revenge. He opened a decorated box, took out a lump of wax and modelled it into the shape of a crocodile. And as he worked he sang magical words. Then he turned to his loyal servant.

"Tomorrow, when the boyfriend leaves the gazebo and goes down to the pool to bathe, throw this crocodile into the water after him."

The servant, who was very frightened by what he had seen and heard, agreed at once to do as his master had ordered.

The next day the wife and her boyfriend met in secret in the gazebo. But when the man went to bathe in the pool the servant threw the wax crocodile into the water after him. And the small wax crocodile grew into a living beast with cruel teeth, small, mean eyes and a thrashing tail. The crocodile seized the horrified boyfriend in its powerful jaws and dragged him under the water.

Webaoner spent the next seven days working away from home at the palace. And all that time his wife's boyfriend was trapped under the water with the crocodile. On the eighth day Webaoner returned home and the king of Egypt went with him.

Standing on the edge of the calm pool, Webaoner called to the crocodile. The water bubbled and foamed and surged, and out of the depths came the enormous crocodile with the unhappy boyfriend twitching in its jaws. The crocodile placed the shivering man on the grassy bank. Then Webaoner bent down and, totally fearless, picked up the crocodile. It shrank and turned back to wax in his hands.

Webaoner told the king all about his wife and her boyfriend. The king thought for a moment, then gave his judgement. The man had lived under the water for seven days. He now belonged to the crocodile. At once the wax figure came back to life and, picking up the man, slithered into the water, never to be seen again.

THE LOST CHARM:
THE STORY TOLD BY PRINCE BAUEFRE

Once upon a time Egypt was ruled by King Snefru, the richest man in the whole world. He had everything that anyone could wish for - piles of silver and gold, granaries filled with grain and warehouses filled with wine. He had a fleet of wooden ships, three splendid pyramids and many sons. But inside his magnificent palace he had grown bored. He wandered from room to room looking for something, anything, which would entertain him. Finally he summoned his high priest and asked his advice. The high priest came up with a wonderful plan.

Snefru made his way to the palace lake. Here a golden throne had been prepared for him. Sitting outside Snefru could admire his beautiful country. The sparkling blue water and the clear blue sky, the sandy shore, the green fields and grey mountains beyond. But Snefru's attention was firmly fixed on the lake. Here twenty of Egypt's most beautiful girls were rowing up and down using oars made from ebony and gold.

Out on the sunlit water the girls rowed with a slow, steady stroke. They sang as they rowed, their hair swinging in rhythm with their songs. Never had Snefru been so happy. But suddenly the tranquillity of the moment was broken. The leading girl cried out in distress. A precious fish-shaped charm had fallen from her hair and was lost in the water. The rowers laid down their oars in confusion; the boats stopped moving and the happy voices faded away. The king quickly promised to buy a new charm but the girl was sobbing and could not be comforted. Once again Snefru sent for his high priest.

The high priest spoke just one magical word and the waters of the lake became solid. Carefully folding one side of the lake back onto the other, he reached down and collected the charm, which he could see lying on a piece of broken pot on the lakebed. A second command turned the lake back to water, and the girls started to row and sing again.

THE MAGICIAN DJEDI:
THE STORY TOLD BY PRINCE HARDJEDEF

Prince Hardjedef stood up to tell his story. He did not tell his father about things that had happened in the past. He spoke about a magician who was still alive.

"A man named Djedi lives in a village not far away. He is one hundred and ten years old, but he eats five hundred loaves of bread and half a cow every day, and he drinks one hundred jugs of beer. This man can rejoin a head that has been cut off a body so that a dead animal becomes alive again. And he can tame a lion so that it walks behind him like a cat!"

Khufu was fascinated by his son's story. He ordered Prince Hardjedef to bring the magician to him at once.

Hardjedef sailed to the village of the magician. He found the wise old man lying on a mat in the courtyard of his house. A servant squatted beside his master, rubbing his master's bald scalp with scented oils. A second servant rubbed the magician's feet. Hardjedef was amazed. He knew that Djedi was incredibly old, but he looked like a fit young man.

The prince hailed the old man politely.

43

"Greetings, O great magician. I have come to welcome you to the palace of my father, King Khufu. There you may eat the finest of foods, and drink the best of wines."

The old man addressed the prince with equal respect.

"Welcome Hardjedef, beloved son of Khufu. May your father always praise you."

Then the prince held out his hands and pulled the old man gently to his feet. Linking arms they walked together to the harbour. Djedi embarked on the royal boat and sailed in splendid style to the palace.

King Khufu could hardly wait to see the magician. Rushing to the great pillared hall, quite forgetting his manners in his eagerness, he fired a question at the old man.

"Is it true what they say, that you can rejoin a severed head?"

"Yes, my king, I can."

In great excitement Khufu ordered that a prisoner be brought from the jail, so that he might be beheaded and brought back to life. But Djedi stopped him.

"There is no need to execute anyone, my king. Our law forbids murder. Let us kill an animal instead."

And so a goose was brought into the great pillared

45

hall, and its head was cut off. Its body was placed on the west side of the hall, and its head was placed on the east side. In a deep voice, Djedi uttered a magical spell. And at once the body of the goose stood up and waddled towards its head, while the head started to roll towards its body. The two halves of the bird met in the middle of the hall and were joined, so that the goose was whole and alive and cackling again.

Khufu watched, open-mouthed, as Djedi repeated his trick first with a long-legged bird and then, most impressively, with a full-grown bull. Finally, as an encore, a roaring lion was dragged in, and the magician showed that he could tame the savage beast with just one word, so that it walked behind him, gentle as a kitten.

Khufu was very pleased with what he had seen. He gave the magician Djedi a house, a generous ration of food and beer, and a tomb near his own pyramid.

ABOUT THE THREE MAGICAL STORIES

King Khufu was a real king of Egypt. He is famous because he built the Great Pyramid at Giza, the one surviving monument of the "Seven Wonders of the World". His son, Prince Khaefre, tells our first story. Khaefre also became king of Egypt; he was the builder of the Great Sphinx. The other two storytelling princes are real people too, but neither of them became king. Old King Snefru is the father of Khufu. He is famous for building not one but three huge pyramids.

Khufu's Great Pyramid was built by a skilled workforce of 20,000 free men. These workers were treated with great respect. They lived in a special village near the pyramid building site. Here they were given food, drink, housing and medical care.

Khufu built his pyramid because he wanted his mummy to be protected for ever. He also wanted to show that he was the richest ruler in the world. We are not sure why Egyptian kings chose the pyramid shape for their tombs. They might have thought that a ramp-like building would help the spirit of the dead king travel into the sky. They may even have thought that the straight sides of the pyramid looked a bit like the sun's rays, particularly when the shiny, white pyramid sparkled in the sunlight. The shape might also have been connected with the story of the creation of the world - the pyramid rising out of the flat desert may have looked like Atum's island.

Egypt is today a safe, crocodile-free zone. But in ancient times the banks of the River Nile were dangerous places, with hungry crocodiles lurking in the reeds. People who had to go down to the river to fetch water or wash clothes had to be very careful. The Egyptians feared crocodiles but they also respected their strength. They worshipped a crocodile god named Sobek, and people who were eaten by crocodiles were regarded as lucky.

WHAT DO YOU THINK?

1. Why do you think King Khufu built his Great Pyramid?

2. Who was King Snefru?

3. Why did Prince Hardjedef sail to meet Djedi? Would he not have been quicker travelling by chariot?

4. Why did the magician Djedi stop Khufu from cutting off a man's head?

6

THE STORY OF THE SHIPWRECKED SAILOR

The great ship had at last reached its port. The gangplank was lowered and the sailors were hurrying ashore in good humour, eager to spend their wages. The long voyage had made them thirsty for beer and hungry for fresh bread and meat.

But not everyone was rushing to leave the boat. Huddled in his cabin, the High Official sat silent and unmoving on his stool. He had failed in his mission, and was now very frightened indeed. How would the king react to his failure? What would happen to him?

A servant approached the High Official and spoke to him kindly:

"Cheer up, my lord. We have reached home safely. You should be thanking the gods for our good luck. We have survived a long and difficult journey, and have travelled all the way from Nubia without any loss of life amongst the crew. Now, listen to me. You must pull yourself together. Have a wash and a shave, and make yourself look decent. Prepare yourself to face the king

49

and be ready to answer his questions."

The High Official made no move. And the talkative servant grew irritated with him:

"Do as you like then, it is up to you. Do nothing to save yourself. It is a waste of my valuable time talking to you. But remember, disasters can come right in the end. Something similar happened to me once. Listen, while I tell you my story:

"A long time ago I sailed on the great green sea in a massive ship crewed by a hundred and twenty of Egypt's best sailors. A fine, lion-hearted bunch of men they were, the bravest in the whole land.

"For many days our voyage went well and we made good time with a strong wind behind us. Then a violent storm broke while we were far away from land. The heavens grew dark and angry, and the sea threw up huge waves, each larger than the last. Our boat rocked dangerously, and there was nothing we could do to save ourselves. We clung to the ropes in fear until one enormous wave smashed down on us, snapping the mast and bringing it thundering down on the deck.

"That was the end. The ship sank, and the rest of the crew were drowned. I was the only survivor. The waves carried me to an island. I was washed up on a sandy shore and I managed to crawl up the beach to the shelter of a grove of trees. And there I lay for three days and three nights.

"On the fourth day I was able to stagger to my feet and look around for something to eat, for I was starving. I was very lucky. I discovered that I was on an island filled with all kinds of tempting food. I found grapes and fine vegetables. There were many kinds of figs, and cucumbers as tasty as those picked from the best gardens. There were plump fish swimming in the sea, and fat fowl sitting in the trees. I ate and ate until I could eat no more.

"Then I heard it. A low rumbling, thundering noise. The earth shook, the trees splintered, and I fell down and hid my face in fear. I thought that another enormous wave was about to carry me out to sea, and I clung to the ground in panic.

"When I gained enough courage to look up, I found that I was facing something far worse than a massive wave. A gigantic golden snake was slithering towards me, his head raised up, as if about to strike. This was no ordinary snake. He was incredibly long. His eyebrows were formed from precious blue stone, and his beard was long and impressive.

"The snake noticed me cowering on the ground and hissed:

'Hissss. Sssss. Who brought you here, ssssailor? If you do not tell me at once, I will kill you. Sssss'

"Trembling with fear I tried to make a sensible reply, but I could only stutter. The snake listened in silence, then lowered his magnificent head and picked me up in his mouth. He carried me to his nest and placed me gently on the ground. Then he spoke to me again, this time with kindness.

'Hissss. Sssss. Who brought you here, ssssailor, to my ssssecret island in the green sssssea? Sssspeak to me. Sssss. I will not hurt you.'

"And I answered him, telling him all about the magnificent ship, the terrible storm, the enormous wave and the death of my friends.

"He spoke to me again.

'Hissss. Sssss. Don't be frightened, ssssailor. Don't tremble and shake. The godsssss have ssssaved you, and have brought you to this ghosssst island. It is an island full of good thingssss and I will look after you. Sssss. You will live here for four monthsssss. Then a ship will come from Egypt, crewed by your friendsssss. You will go home with them and will live a long and happy life in your hometown. Sssss'

"Then the snake grew sad, and a large tear splashed from his eye.

'Hissss. Sssss. I also have a sssstory of disasssster to tell, but my sssstory has an unhappy ending. Many yearssss ago I lived on thissss island with my wife and my brotherssss and their wivessss and children. There were sssseventy-five of us giant sssnakessss plussss my much-loved little daughter. We were one big, happy family, and life wassss good. Hissss. But one day, while I wassss away hunting for food, a sssstar fell from the sssssky. It burned up our village, and when I returned home everyone wassss dead. Sssss. I wanted to die when I ssssaw what had happened, but I had to live on, alone. Now I tell you thissss. If you are brave you will sssssee your home and hug your children and kissss your wife once again. Hissss. Sssss.'

"I felt a sudden wave of happiness wash over me. I was not going to be eaten - I would see my home and family again. I spoke without thinking:

'I will tell the king of Egypt about your kindness to me. I will send you precious oils, and fine perfumes, and ships full of treasure. Everyone in the world will hear of your goodness.'

"Hearing this the great snake hissed with laughter.

'Hissss. Sssss. Don't be ssssilly. I know that you could never afford to give me ssssuch sssplendid giftssss. I am the Lord of Punt, and I have all the oilssss and precioussss perfumessss that I need right here on my island. Jusssst make sure that my deedssss are known in your land - that will be reward enough for me. Sssss. This island will vanish when you leave it. When you have left here, you can never come back. Sssss.'

"Everything happened exactly as the snake had said. The ship came. I made my farewell, bowing low, and the great snake gave me precious gifts; perfumes, oils, eye-paint, giraffe tails, elephant tusks, long-tailed monkeys and much, much more. I loaded these presents onto the ship and we sailed north, to Egypt. Two months later we reached the royal palace and I gave my gifts to the king. And this is how my disaster became a triumph."

As he finished his long story the servant looked encouragingly at the High Official. But the Official was not brave enough to face up to his problems and make the best of a bad situation. He spoke for the first time, with great bitterness:

"Do not try to help me my friend. My doom is come."

He refused to leave the ship and continued to sit huddled on his chair, quaking with fear.

ABOUT THE SHIPWRECKED SAILOR

This is a confusing story (told by the snake) inside a story (told by the sailor) inside a story. None of the people in any of the stories is given a name, which just makes the whole thing all the more confusing.

The High Official has sailed back from Nubia (modern Sudan), the land directly to the south of Egypt. We do not know where the giant snake's disappearing island was, but Punt was a real, far distant trading post somewhere on the Red Sea coast.

The Egyptians were exceptionally good at sailing on the River Nile, but they liked to be able to see land from their boats. They were not very keen on sea sailing, as they had no real means of knowing where they were. This meant that any sea voyage became an exciting and sometimes uncomfortable adventure.

WHAT DO YOU THINK?

1. Why is the High Official so upset?

2. Do you think that the Egyptians feared snakes?

3. Can you describe the giant snake?

7

THE ADVENTURES OF SINUHE

This story is told by Sinuhe, a friend of the King of Egypt.

One day a terrible thing happened. The King of Egypt was murdered in his palace! The whole land went into shock. The nobles cried in their mansions and the people wept in the streets.

When I heard about the king's death I felt very scared. My heart pounded and I trembled from head to foot. I knew that Egypt was no longer safe. I had to run away.

I travelled through the desert, heading for the River Nile. At suppertime I reached the harbour and stole a boat to cross the river. I kept on walking until I reached the border. Here I squatted in a bush, hiding from the border guards. By now I had walked a long way and I was feeling very tired.

That night I left the safety of my bush and continued my travels. But then, in the hot foreign desert, I collapsed. I could walk no further. My lips were blistered and my throat dry. I lay down and closed my eyes and waited for death to take me.

At that terrible moment, just when I thought my end had come, I heard the sound of mooing cows. Sitting up and opening my eyes I saw a group of nomads. Their leader gave me water and boiled milk and took me to live with his tribe.

The leader of the nomads took a great fancy to me. He allowed me to marry his beautiful daughter, and gave me a good patch of land to live on. There were fat figs on the trees, plump grapes on the vines, combs of sweet honey and baskets full of olives. The trees were heavy with fruits, the fields were ripe with grain and there were many kinds of cattle. Every day, bread was baked for me, wine was brought to me and meats were cooked for me.

Here I spent many happy years with my wife and family. I watched my baby sons grow into strong men. My tent became a resting place for weary travellers. I gave water to the thirsty, directions to the lost and help to those who had been robbed.

One day a man came to my tent to challenge me to a fight. He was a huge, rough man, very tall and very strong. He wanted to beat me and steal my goods and my cattle. He had decided to ruin my life - I don't know why. Perhaps he hated me because I was a foreigner - an Egyptian living outside Egypt. I knew that I could not let this man beat me. I had to prove my bravery.

That evening I strung my bow, checked my arrows and sharpened my weapons. I didn't sleep much that night - I was too worried about the next day's fight.

When morning came I left the safety of my tent. Only then did I realise that many people had come to watch our fight. Most of them were on my side, and that made me feel good.

I stood shaking with fear. The huge man raised his bow and shot his arrows into the air. By some miracle, all the arrows missed me. Then, as my enemy charged forward, I shot him in the neck. He screamed and fell forward onto his face, breaking his nose with a loud crunch. Seizing his battleaxe, I cut off his head. As the crowd cheered, I gave a great shout of triumph.

Many years passed and I grew old and weak. I wanted to return to Egypt but I was scared. Perhaps the king would punish me, or even kill me, because I had run away.

The king of Egypt heard of my adventures and realised that I was ready to come home. He sent me letters and gifts, and his children sent me presents. The king begged me to return to Egypt.

When I received his kind messages I was overcome

with emotion. I threw myself to the ground and cried with joy. Then, I started to plan my return.

I gave all my land and property to my eldest son. Then I started my homeward journey, guided by my faithful nomad friends. When I reached the Egyptian border an escort came to meet me. I boarded a tall ship and set sail for the palace, leaving my desert life behind me. And at daybreak I reached the capital of Egypt.

At last I saw great stone sphinxes that guard the palace entrance. I was taken to the throne room and found myself standing before my king. I fell to the ground in a panic, and lay there quaking with fear. His majesty must have thought that I was an idiot. He had to order a servant to pick me up and hold me to stop me from falling while he spoke.

"Welcome home Sinuhe. You have returned to Egypt after many years abroad. You were a young man when you left, but now you are old. Do not be frightened of me. Do not worry that you will be punished for running away many years ago. I do not wish to harm you."

The queen and the royal princesses rushed in to greet me. They stopped in shock when they saw me, because my beard and the layers of desert dirt made me unrecognisable. They took me by the hand and led me into a nearby house. This was a house of great luxury; it had a cool bathroom and mirrors, linen clothing, perfumes and servants to look after me. I was washed, and felt lighter as the desert dirt drained away with the water. I was shaved and my hair was cut. Then I was dressed in the finest linen and perfumed with the sweetest scent. That night, I slept in a bed for the first time in years.

The king gave me a house, a garden and a regular ration of food. Best of all, I was given a small stone pyramid in the royal cemetery.

ABOUT THE ADVENTURES OF SINUHE

Sinuhe's adventure is meant to confuse us into thinking that it is a true story. But Sinuhe never existed and his story is fiction not fact.

Sinuhe's story tells us that Egypt is the best land in the world. Every Egyptian wants to come home to die. Sinuhe is prepared to abandon all the luxuries of his desert life - including his children - in order to return to Egypt.

The king who is murdered at the beginning of this story is a real king of Egypt named Amenemhat I. He was really murdered, too, but no one knows who did the terrible deed. It is an ancient murder mystery.

Sinuhe was so frightened that he fled from Egypt, crossing the Sinai land bridge into southern Canaan.

In Canaan Sinuhe lived in a tent not a house. He had no bed, no bathroom, no fresh linen and no barber to shave his beard. Cleanliness was very important to the Egyptians, and they looked down on people who did not have their own high standards of hygiene. When Sinuhe finally returned home, the first thing he did was to have a good scrub in the bathtub!

WHAT DO YOU THINK?

1. Why do you think that Sinuhe ran away from Egypt?

2. How did Sinuhe's life in Canaan differ from his life in Egypt?

3. The entrance to the Egyptian royal palace is guarded by two stone sphinxes. Do you know what a sphinx is?

4. Egyptian men and women wore clothes made of linen. Do you know which plant is grown to make linen?

8

THE PRINCE, THE DOG, THE SNAKE AND THE CROCODILE

Once upon a time there lived an old king. This king had everything that a man could want; health, wealth, a beautiful palace and a loving young queen. Yet he was sad because he had no child, and he longed for a child more than anything in the world. The king prayed that his queen might have a baby and the gods agreed to grant his wish. The queen gave birth to a son and the king was filled with happiness.

The time came for the Seven Hathors to decide the baby's fate. The palace was hushed as they leaned over the crib and spoke.

"This Prince will meet his death through a dog, or through a snake, or maybe through a crocodile."

The king instantly plunged into a deep gloom. He loved his baby son more than anything in the world, and he did not want him to die young.

Determined to protect the baby, the king had a stone house built far away in the desert. The house was filled

with expensive furniture and food and drink taken from the palace kitchens. Here the prince would grow up safe from dogs, snakes and crocodiles. He would never be allowed to play outside and so would never come face to face with his fate.

The years flew by and the pretty baby grew into a fine boy. But the young prince was very lonely and he longed for a companion. One day he was sitting on the roof of his house and he saw a man walk by, followed by a greyhound. The prince was fascinated - he had never seen a dog before. Excited, he called for his attendant, and demanded to know just what the strange four-legged creature could be.

"It is a greyhound dog, my prince."

"Have one just like it brought to me, now!"

Troubled, the attendant went straight to the king. And the king did not know what to do. He had no wish to stop his son enjoying himself, but he wanted to protect him from his fate. Reluctantly he ordered that a small puppy be brought to the prince.

Many more years passed and the fine boy became a fully-grown, handsome man. Then the prince, who was as clever as he was handsome, sent a message to his father.

"Why should I sit here all alone? I cannot avoid my

fate. Let me go free so that I may live as I wish until the gods decide to kill me."

The king could see the sense of this argument. So a splendid chariot was prepared for the prince, equipped with an impressive range of weapons. And a servant was appointed to accompany him on his travels. Eagerly the prince set off, free at last. And his faithful greyhound, now a full-grown dog, went with him.

The prince travelled northwards over the desert, following no particular path. And at last he came to the far-off land of Naharin.

Now the King of Naharin had only one child, a daughter. His daughter was more beautiful than any other woman in the world and she was as sweet and kind as she was beautiful. Her father loved her deeply. He felt that only the most noble and athletic of princes should be her husband. So he built a tall stone tower. And here at the high window the beautiful princess stood alone, looking down on the world below.

The King of Naharin summoned her would-be boyfriends to the base of the tower. They listened as the king spoke:

"Whoever jumps up to my daughter's window will win her hand in marriage."

The princes immediately started to leap upwards, trying to reach the high window. They did this day after day, for they were each determined to win the hand of the beautiful princess.

Three months passed, and the young men continued to jump. Eventually the Egyptian prince passed by on his travels and stopped, fascinated by the high tower and the jumping princes. The princes made the newcomer feel very welcome. They took him to their lodgings, bathed him, rubbed him with oils and bandaged his feet, which were covered in blisters. Curious, they asked where he had come from. The prince quickly made up a story:

"I am the son of an Egyptian chariot driver. When my mother died my father chose a new wife, a stepmother to look after me. But she hated me. So I ran away from home."

The princes felt sorry for the stranger. They hugged him and begged him to feel at home with them.

The prince just had to ask: "Why do your spend every day leaping up towards that window, lads?"

And they told him the whole story of the King of Naharin, his beautiful daughter and her impossible window. The Egyptian was eager to try to win the hand of the fair princess but he couldn't; his sore feet hurt too much. So he was forced to stand by and watch as his new friends made their daily jumps. But unknown to him, high in her tower, the princess had her eye on the newcomer. For he was as handsome as she was beautiful, and she had decided that he would be her husband.

A few days later the prince's feet were fully healed. With one mighty jump he sailed through the air and reached the window of the princess of Naharin. She was delighted. She kissed him, and hugged him and would not let him go. Meanwhile her attendants rushed to tell the king that his daughter's husband was found.

"Which high-born boy has reached my princess?" the king demanded.

His face fell as he realised that his precious daughter had been won, not by a noble prince or count, but by the lowly son of an Egyptian charioteer.

"Do you really expect me to give my daughter to an Egyptian tramp? Make him go away, at once!"

The attendants hurried back to the tower, and ordered the prince to leave Naharin. But the princess heard their words, and grew angry.

"I swear, if this man is taken away from me I will not eat and I will not drink. I willll die, straightaway."

Trembling, the attendants returned to the King of Naharin. The king thought for a moment, then sent men to kill the Egyptian. But again the princess realised what was happening, and again she made a vow.

"If this man is killed, I too will be dead before sunset. I will not live a single hour without him."

Hearing these words, the King of Naharin realised that his daughter had outsmarted him. She must really be in love. He summoned the couple and gave his blessing to their marriage. They were given a house, fields, cattle and all sorts of good things as wedding presents.

After many days the Egyptian prince told his wife the truth about his fate.

"I have been told that I will be killed by one of three animals: a snake, a dog or a crocodile."

Alarmed by this news, the new bride at once demanded that the prince's faithful greyhound be killed. But the prince refused to listen:

"How stupid you are. I have raised this dog from a puppy. He is a lovely dog - my best friend in the whole world. He will never harm me."

The wife, however, was unconvinced, and she started to watch her husband closely from that day onwards.

Now, unknown to the prince, the crocodile that was to be his fate had followed him from Egypt and was lurking in a pond in the village next to his house. There it was stuck, because a strong and violent imp also lived in the pond. The imp would not let the crocodile leave the water to kill the prince, and the crocodile would not let the imp leave the water to stroll around the village. Every day, as soon as the sun rose, the crocodile and the imp fought each other tooth and nail.

The next day was a holiday. The prince spent the day eating and drinking in his house; this so tired him out that he fell asleep that night as soon as his head touched his headrest. Luckily his wife was still alert. She filled a bowl with red wine and put it on the floor. Then she sat and watched her sleeping husband.

Suddenly, without warning, a long, dark snake slithered out of a hole in the bedroom wall. It had planned to bite the young prince and kill him. But instead it drank from the wine bowl, and became sleepy and confused.

As the snake dozed on the floor the wife crept forward and hacked it to pieces with a knife. This woke the prince, who demanded to know what was going on. The wife was able to show him the pieces of snake, dripping with snake blood.

"Look, you have been saved from one of your three fates. Now there are only two fates left!"

The next day the prince went for a stroll round the village. Naturally, he took his faithful greyhound with him. But his wife stayed at home because she was tired after her nighttime adventures.

Suddenly, and very scarily, the dog began to speak in a gruff voice.

"I am your fate and I am going to kill you. Woof!"

Hearing this, the prince took to his heels, running away from the dog, straight towards the pond. Jumping into the water he had just one second to think himself safe before the crocodile seized him in its powerful jaws.

To his absolute horror, the crocodile also spoke.

"I am your fate! I have followed you from Egypt to kill you. But for many months now I have been fighting the imp that lives in this lake. If I let you go, you must help me to catch the imp that torments me every day."

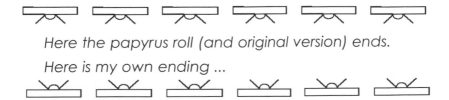

Here the papyrus roll (and original version) ends.

Here is my own ending ...

73

Reluctantly the prince agreed to help the crocodile catch the imp. Instantly the crocodile dropped the prince and seized the dog instead. The crocodile plunged back under the water and the dog was drowned. And this saved the prince from his second fate.

The next day the imp returned to the pond and started to fight again with the crocodile. But the bad-tempered imp did not know that the prince and his wife were waiting to capture him. The brave wife walked to the water's edge, and called to the imp.

"Hey, Mr Ugly, I bet you can't catch me."

The imp stopped fighting and looked at the crocodile. Who was she calling ugly?

"Yes, you with the blue lumpy face and nasty green body. I bet you can't catch me."

That did it. The imp jumped straight out of the water, only to find himself trapped in a fishing net thrown by the prince. He struggled for a time, and then lay still, panting. The prince stuffed the imp into an empty beer jar, and sealed it up tight. Then he threw the jar and the imp into the river and watched them float away to sea.

The prince had kept his part of the bargain. But could he trust the crocodile to keep his? Nervously he returned to the pond and called to the crocodile in the water.

"I have got rid of the imp for you. Now you can keep your promise. Go back to Egypt and leave me in peace."

But the crocodile rose up out of the water, laughing in a mean and frightening way.

"Thank you for removing the imp from my pond. It was very kind of you. Now, of course, I am going to kill you. I am your last fate and you can't escape from me."

Hearing these words the prince grew pale. His legs shook so much it was impossible to run away. He closed his eyes, and prayed to his gods.

Suddenly there was a bloodcurdling yell. Quickly the prince opened his eyes. He found the crocodile twitching at his feet, a large harpoon stuck in its throat. Next to him stood his wife, a harpoon rope in her hand and a satisfied grin on her face.

As the crocodile choked and died the prince felt truly free for the first time in his life.

ABOUT THE PRINCE, THE DOG, THE SNAKE AND THE CROCODILE

The ancient version of this story was written on a roll of papyrus. Unfortunately it has been damaged at the most exciting point. Did the prince survive the crocodile and the dog? Or did he get eaten? We will never know, but I have added my own ending to make the story complete.

The beginning of the story is a bit like the fairy story Sleeping Beauty. Here the baby is a boy not a girl, and he is visited by seven forms of the goddess Hathor who tell the baby's fate. The Seven Hathors are not mean - they just say what they think will happen. They are not always right. Luckily, the prince marries a clever wife who is able to help him. The middle of the story, where the beautiful princess is locked in her high tower, might remind you of the fairy story Rapunzel.

This story was written quite late in Egyptian history. We can tell this because the prince does not walk out of Egypt, or sail by boat. He has a comfortable journey travelling by chariot. The Egyptians did not use horse-drawn chariots until the New Kingdom (the time of Tutankhamen and Ramesses the Great).

WHAT DO YOU THINK?

1. Why did the king of Egypt make his son live all alone in the house in the desert?

2. What were the three fates that threatened the prince?

3. Why did the princes spend all their time jumping in front of the princess's tower?

4. I have written my own ending to the story. Can you write one?

9

THE STORY OF TRUTH AND FALSEHOOD

Once upon a time there were two brothers. Truth was a good, simple man but his brother Falsehood was a liar who could not be trusted.

One day Truth borrowed a dagger from his brother Falsehood. It was a useful dagger made of sharp flint with a fine bone handle, but it was not very expensive. So Truth did not think that Falsehood would mind too much when he dropped the dagger in the river and lost it.

Falsehood did mind, though. He sent the police to arrest his brother, and had him dragged before the court. There he told a string of humongous lies:

"My dagger was huge, easily as big as a mountain. It had a massive copper blade as long as the River Nile and an enormous carved handle made from more than one hundred trees. It was incredibly expensive - the best thing that I ever owned. I loved it so much. And now Truth has lost my precious dagger on purpose, and I am really upset. You must punish Truth for his crime. You must make him blind in both eyes. Then you must order him to work as my doorkeeper."

The court was very impressed by Falsehood's fine words. They believed him and punished Truth as he asked.

Truth started his new job as doorkeeper at Falsehood's house. It was his responsibility to check all the visitors who passed in and out. He worked hard at his new job and did not complain. But the sight of his good brother sitting patiently by his door irritated Falsehood. He decided to have Truth murdered. That way he would never have to see him again.

Falsehood ordered his servants to lead Truth into the desert and leave him in the place where the wild lions hunted so that he would be killed and eaten. The servants did lead Truth into the desert, but then they let him escape because they liked Truth very much and they hated his brother Falsehood. The servants returned home and lied, telling Falsehood that they had seen the largest of the hungry lions eat every bit of Truth.

The next day a fine lady came out of her house accompanied by her servants. She caught sight of Truth sleeping under a bush in the desert, and fell in love with him. The lady told her servants to pick Truth up and carry him to her house, and that very night she married him.

79

Soon Truth and the fine lady had a baby boy. But the lady did not treat her blind husband well. She made him work as the doorkeeper in his own house.

The son born to Truth and the fine lady was a wonderful child; he was tall, healthy, and strong. At school he was best in his class at writing and fighting. But his school friends were jealous of his success and they teased him in a very mean way.

"Whose son are you? You don't have a father like we do."

The boy was very upset by his friends' words. He went to his mother, and asked her to name his father. Much to his surprise she told him that his father was the blind doorkeeper who sat by their door.

The boy was astonished at this news. He went to his father and hugged him. He brought him a comfortable chair and a footstool. He gave him good food to eat, and beer to drink. Then he asked him a question.

"Tell me who blinded you, father. I want to punish that person."

Truth told his son the whole sad story.

The boy was determined to punish his evil uncle Falsehood. He thought long and hard, and eventually came up with a good plan. He packed ten loaves of

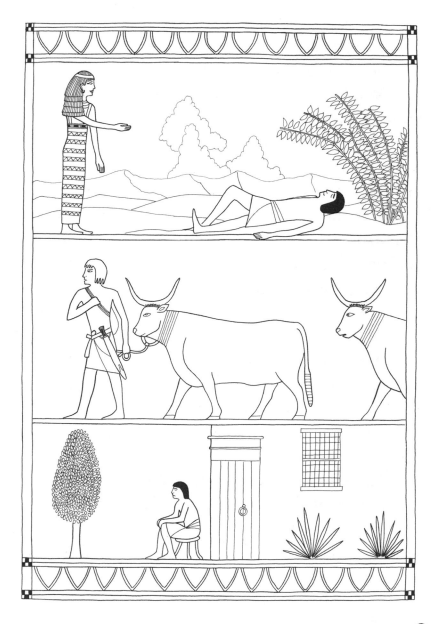

bread, a walking stick, a pair of sandals, a jug of water and a sword. Then he fetched a beautiful ox from his mother's field, and walked with it to his uncle's farm.

The boy spoke to the herdsman in charge of Falsehood's cattle.

"You can have my bread and my walking stick, my water, my sword and my sandals, because I do not need them. But please look after my ox until I collect him."

The herdsman was very happy with this bargain, and gladly agreed to care for the ox for as long as the boy wanted. The ox was put in a field with Falsehood's cattle and the boy walked away.

A few days later, while Falsehood was out walking, he caught sight of the beautiful ox. He ordered the herdsman to bring the animal to him; he wanted to kill it and eat it. But the herdsman refused.

"It is not my ox sir, and I cannot give it to you."

"Surely I can have this ox? You can give one of my fine cows to its owner, in its place."

And so it was done. Falsehood killed and ate the beautiful ox that belonged to the son of Truth.

The young boy soon learned that his uncle had killed and eaten his beautiful ox. Quickly he returned to the herdsman and demanded the return of his animal. Of course this was impossible. Sadly, the herdsman explained what had happened, and offered him any one of Falsehood's cows in its place. But the boy insisted that he wanted his own ox. No other animal would do.

"None of these cows is as big as my ox was. My ox was as big as the land of Egypt. If my ox stood on the bank of the Nile its tail would brush the papyrus marshes in the north while one horn would rest on the eastern mountain, and one on the west."

The herdsman laughed at the boy's exaggeration.

"That is impossible. No one has an ox as big as the land of Egypt. No ox could ever be that big."

The boy called the police and demanded that Falsehood be dragged before the court.

At first the judges were not impressed with the boy's claim to have owned an enormous ox as big as the land of Egypt.

"What you have described is obviously impossible. We have never seen an ox as large as the one you describe."

But the boy would not shut up.

"I see. You do not believe that I had an ox that was as big as the land of Egypt. But you do believe that Falsehood here once owned a huge dagger as big as a mountain with a copper blade as long as the River Nile

83

and an enormous carved handle made from more than one hundred trees?"

This made the judges shut up and think. Then the boy told the judges who he was and what he wanted.

"You must now judge between Truth and Falsehood. I am the son of Truth who has done no wrong, and I have come to avenge my blind father."

Falsehood was astonished to hear this, because he honestly believed that a wild lion had eaten his brother in the desert many years before. He spoke to the judges:

"Truth is dead. I swear before you all, that if you can find Truth alive you can blind me in both eyes and I will become his doorkeeper."

This was just what the boy had been waiting to hear. He led the judges to his mother's house and there was his father, alive and sitting as always by the door.

So Falsehood received the most severe of punishments. He was beaten one hundred times for lying, and blinded in both eyes. And now Falsehood was made to work as the doorkeeper in the house of Truth.

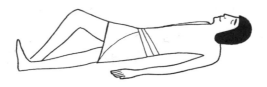

ABOUT THE STORY OF TRUTH AND FALSEHOOD

This story shows that in ancient Egypt, as today, lying was not a good thing. Falsehood lies to the court and gets his brother into serious trouble. It takes a long time, but eventually he is punished for his bad behaviour. It is funny that the one thing that Falsehood honestly thinks is true - that Truth has been eaten by a lion - turns out to be a lie.

The ancient Egyptians had a police force called the Medjay. It was their duty to protect the king and guard the palaces, temples and tombs against robbers. The people arrested by the Medjay would be tried before a court. Punishments were harsh for those found guilty; they might be beaten, banished to the mines, or even executed. Not many prisoners were blinded though, because the Egyptians liked their criminals to be able to do a full day's work.

We are not told the names of Truth's wife and Truth's son. We can guess that the son had a name that showed his goodness - perhaps something like "Brave"? Truth's wife is not a very nice lady - she rescues Truth from the desert, but then makes him work in her house. Perhaps she was called "Selfish" or "Mean"?

WHAT DO YOU THINK?

1. Can you remember how Falsehood described his lost dagger?

2. What did the boy give to the herdsman?

3. Did the boy really have a massive ox?

4. Why did Falsehood think that Truth was dead?

10

THE BATTLE OF KADESH

This is the story of the battle fought by the great King of Egypt Ramesses II, in the fifth year of his reign.

The mighty army had marched northeastwards, heading for the walled city of Kadesh. Here they were going to fight against Egypt's strongest enemy - the army of the Hittites.

The Egyptians had made good progress and had stopped to camp for the night. As King Ramesses sat on a golden throne in his tent he heard a scuffling noise. Two of his soldiers appeared, dragging two strangers with them. The strangers had been caught lurking on the outskirts of the camp.

Ramesses questioned the new arrivals.

"Who are you, and where have you come from?"

"Do not hurt us, sir! We are just two simple soldiers. We fought for the Hittite king, but we have decided to change sides. We have decided to serve the noble King of Egypt instead."

Pleased by this answer, Ramesses questioned the men again.

"But where is the Hittite army? We have been marching for days and have not seen any sign of them. Are they hidden nearby?"

"Oh no, sir. The Hittite army is camped many miles away. They are too frightened to come closer because they know that you will beat them in the great battle that is to come."

Ramesses was delighted with this news. He could march straight to Kadesh and capture the city before the Hittites arrived. He went to bed and enjoyed a good night's sleep.

Unfortunately for Ramesses, the two strangers were liars. They were secret agents working for the King of the Hittites. Their mission was to fool the King of Egypt and stop him making ready for battle. Actually, the Hittites had already arrived at Kadesh and were hiding behind the city ready to ambush the Egyptians.

The next day the Egyptian army continued the march to Kadesh. Eventually they came to the mighty River Orontes. Ramesses decided to split his troops into four divisions. He would lead the first division across the river and set up camp in the wood just outside Kadesh. The second division would follow, while the other two divisions would stay on the far side of the river. And this is what happened. The Egyptian army spread out on either side of the River Orontes. The division led by the king marched ahead and set up camp in the wood. Soon Ramesses was once again sitting on his golden throne in his tent.

Then, once again, there was a scuffling noise outside his tent. A soldier lifted the tent flap and entered, dragging with him two more strangers. With a dry feeling in his throat, Ramesses spoke directly to the prisoners.

"Who exactly are you?"

This time he got a truthful reply.

"Do not hurt us sir! We are secret agents working for the king of the Hittites. He has sent us to spy on you."

"But surely the king of the Hittites is hiding many miles away from here?"

"No! Whoever told you that? The king of the Hittites has already arrived at Kadesh. He has many foot soldiers and many charioteers with him, and all his soldiers have sharpened their weapons. They stand ready for battle behind the old city of Kadesh."

Ramesses had the prisoners dragged away and beaten. Then he called his generals to an emergency meeting.

"We are in a terrible situation. The Hittites are very near, hidden behind the old city of Kadesh. We must prepare for an immediate ambush!"

There was just time to send a swift messenger to summon the remainder of the Egyptian army. Then the Hittites attacked. Soon Ramesses and his men were completely surrounded. Scared, the Egyptian soldiers took one look at the enemy and ran away. Ramesses and his shield bearer were left completely alone.

Ramesses prayed aloud to the great god Amen.

"Oh Amen, my father, help your son Ramesses. I have always served you well. I have built many splendid monuments for you, and filled your temples with great treasure. Now I am relying on you. Help me, and I will serve you with a loving heart until the day that I die. My troops have run away. You are the only one who can help me now."

Far away, in his temple in Egypt, the great god Amen was listening. He spoke, and Ramesses heard his words:

"Go forward my son, and remember that I am always with you. You will triumph over a hundred thousand men, for I am the lord of victory and I will help you."

The fear drained from Ramesses's body. He became strong like the war god Montu, and courageous like Seth the brave. Seizing his weapons, he leapt onto his chariot and charged into battle. The king of Egypt was so fearless and so determined, none of the Hittites dared stand against him. Quickly and ruthlessly Ramesses slayed the entire Hittite army. This is very hard to believe I know, but it is the absolute truth I promise you.

By nightfall the enemy were either dead or had run away, and peace fell on the Egyptian camp. The next day the brave Ramesses was prepared to fight again. But the enemy had had enough. The king of the Hittites sent a messenger to the Egyptian camp, asking for peace. And so it was that Ramesses crushed his Hittite enemies.

ABOUT THE BATTLE OF KADESH

This story tells us about a real battle fought by King Ramesses II against the king of the Hittites at a city in Syria called Kadesh. Although the story is a true one, Ramesses has exaggerated his own part in the battle to make himself seem more important. It is very unlikely that any man, no matter how brave, could actually fight off thousands of enemies single-handed. Ramesses was very proud of this story. He had it copied onto the walls of his temples, his artists carved pictures of the battle, and there was even a famous poem written to celebrate his victory.

Ramesses ruled Egypt for an amazing sixty-six years. He was a very successful king. Outside Egypt he fought many battles to make his empire secure. Back home his workmen built many temples and raised many large stone statues of Ramesses.

WHAT DO YOU THINK?

1. Why did Ramesses think that the enemy were camped a long way from Kadesh?

2. How did he realise that they were hiding nearby?

3. Which god helped Ramesses when he was fighting all alone?

4. Why do you think Ramesses exaggerates his part in the battle?

PEOPLE AND PLACES

AMEN: the warrior god of Thebes

AMENEMHAT I: a king of Egypt

ATUM: the god who made himself at the beginning of
the world

BAUEFRE: a son of King Khufu

BYBLOS: a city on the Mediterranean coast in modern
Lebanon

CANAAN (modern Israel): the land to the northeast of
Egypt

DJEDI: a powerful magician at the court of King Khufu

FALSEHOOD: a bad man, the brother of Truth

GEB: the god of the earth

HARDJEDEF: a son of King Khufu

HATHOR: a goddess, the gentle daughter of Re

HITTITES: the enemy of King Ramesses who lived in the
land that is now Turkey

HORUS: a god, the son of Isis and Osiris

ISIS: the goddess of magic and healing, mother of Horus

KADESH: a walled city in Syria

KHAEFRE: a king of Egypt, son of King Khufu

KHUFU: a king of Egypt, son of King Snefru

MEDJAY: the ancient Egyptian police force

MEMPHIS (near modern Cairo): an important city in
    northern Egypt

MONTU: a god of war

NAHARIN: a far away land in northern Syria

NEPHTHYS: a goddess, the sister of Isis, Osiris and Seth

NILE: the river that flows through the middle of Egypt

NUBIA (modern Sudan): the land to the south of Egypt

NUT: the goddess of the sky

ORONTES: a river in Syria

OSIRIS: the god of the dead, father of Horus

PUNT: a far away land on the Red Sea coast

RAMESSES II "THE GREAT": a king of Egypt

RE: the sun god

SEKHMET: a lion-headed goddess, the fierce daughter
    of Re

SETH: a mean god, the brother of Isis, Osiris and
    Nephthys

SEVEN HATHORS: seven versions of the goddess Hathor
    who could predict the future

SHU: the god of the air

SINAI: the desert area linking Egypt to Canaan

SINUHE: a frightened traveller

SNEFRU: a king of Egypt

SOBEK: a god, who looked like a crocodile

TEFNUT: the goddess of moisture

THEBES (modern Luxor): an important city in southern
 Egypt

TRUTH: a good man, the brother of Falsehood

TUTANKHAMEN: a king of Egypt

WEBAONER: a priest with magical powers

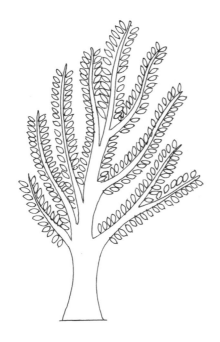
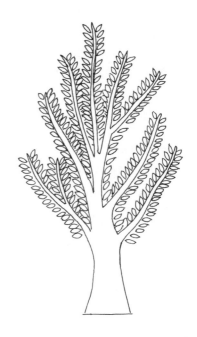

WHAT DO YOU THINK? - ANSWERS

1. THE CREATION OF THE WORLD

1. Why was the River Nile important to the Egyptians?

Egypt is a hot African country with very little rain. The River Nile was important because it provided the people with water to drink, cook, wash, make bricks and grow crops.

2. Why did the Egyptians not need roads?

The Egyptians did not need roads because they travelled by boat. Small boats and rafts carried people up and down the Nile, larger boats carried goods, and huge barges carried the stone used to build the pyramids.

3. What sort of foods do you think the Egyptians ate?

The Egyptians ate a wide range of healthy foods. The main crops were wheat and barley, which they used to make bread, cakes and beer. They also grew beans, vegetables (lettuce, onions and cucumbers) and fruits (melons, dates, grapes and figs). They ate ducks, geese and a huge amount of fish that they could catch in the River Nile. Beef was a very expensive food, but pork and mutton were widely available. The Egyptians had no sugar though; they used honey to sweeten their cakes.

2. HATHOR AND THE RED BEER

1. What did the sun god Re look like?

Re usually looked like a bird of prey (a falcon), or like a man with a falcon's head. But sometimes he looked like a circular sun with wings.

2. Why did the people want to kill Re?

The people wanted to kill Re because they thought that he had grown too old to rule Egypt. They wanted to choose a new king.

3. How did Re stop Hathor from killing all the people?

Re tricked Hathor by pouring red beer over the fields. Hathor thought that the beer was blood. She drank all the beer and grew sleepy and confused. She returned home happy, not knowing that she had failed to kill all the people.

4. What did Egyptian beer taste like?

Egyptian beer was sweet, and so thick that it sometimes had to be drunk through a straw to avoid the lumps!

3. THE STORY OF ISIS AND OSIRIS

1. Why did Seth hate his brother Osiris?

Seth hated Osiris because he was jealous of him. Seth wanted to be king of Egypt.

2. How did Seth trick his brother?

Seth ordered his carpenters to make a splendid box decorated with silver and gold. He told Osiris that the box was a party game, and that he could keep the box if he could fit inside it. Osiris was tricked into lying down in the box, and Seth slammed the lid shut.

3. Why did the Egyptians make mummies?

The Egyptians believed that their spirits or souls would live in their bodies after death. They made their dead bodies into mummies so that they would last forever.

4. Can you guess how much linen cloth was needed to wrap a mummy?

Mummification used up a huge amount of linen. Not everyone could afford new bandages, so the Egyptians became experts in recycling. Mummies were wrapped in old sheets, towels and one sailor was even wrapped in a sail. It would take the same amount of material to wrap one mummy as it would to cover a football pitch.

4. THE QUARREL BETWEEN HORUS AND SETH

1. Why do some gods and goddesses think that Horus should be king of Egypt?

Horus is the son of the dead king Osiris, and so some of the gods and goddesses think that he should be the next king.

2. Why do the other gods and goddesses think that Seth should be king?

Seth has ruled Egypt for many years since the death of Osiris. He is a strong and brave man. Horus just seems too young for the job.

3. Who do you think should be king of Egypt?

This is up to you!

4. What does Isis look like?

A trick question! The Egyptian artists usually showed Isis as a beautiful woman with long dark hair and a long white linen dress. But Isis is a mistress of disguise, and so can easily change her appearance.

5. THREE MAGICAL STORIES

1. Why do you think King Khufu built his Great Pyramid?

Khufu built his pyramid so that it could be the biggest and most splendid tomb in Egypt. It may have been designed as a ramp to allow his spirit to travel to the sky. The straight sides of the pyramid may have looked a bit like the sun's rays, or its shape may have reminded him of the story of the creation of the world.

2. Who was King Snefru?

King Snefru was the father of King Khufu.

3. Why did Prince Hardjedef sail to meet Djedi? Would he not have been quicker travelling by chariot?

No, Hardjedef would not have been quicker travelling by chariot, because Egypt had no chariots and no proper roads when he lived! The first Egyptians travelled by boat because that was the quickest way.

4. Why did the magician Djedi stop Khufu from cutting off a man's head?

Djedi stopped Khufu from cutting off a man's head because murder, even by a king, was against the law.

6. THE STORY OF THE SHIPWRECKED SAILOR

1. Why is the High Official so upset?

The High Official is upset because he has failed to carry out his mission and he may be punished.

2. Do you think that the Egyptians feared snakes?

The Egyptians respected snakes. They knew that snakes could be useful because they killed the rats that stole the grain in the warehouses. One ancient recipe book recommends pushing an onion down a snake hole to stop the snake coming out!

3. Can you describe the giant snake?

The giant snake is very long. It has a golden body, blue eyebrows and a beard, and it can talk. No wonder the sailor is frightened!

7. THE ADVENTURES OF SINUHE

1. Why do you think that Sinuhe ran away from Egypt?

Sinuhe ran away from Egypt because he was frightened by the king's death. He may even have known who killed the king.

2. How did Sinuhe's life in Canaan differ from his life in Egypt?

In Canaan Sinuhe was a married man. He lived in a tent not a house, and he had no bed, no bathroom, no fresh linen and no barber to shave his beard.

3. The entrance to the Egyptian royal palace is guarded by two stone sphinxes. Do you know what a sphinx is?

The sphinx is a mythological beast that has a lion's body topped by a human head or face. In ancient Egypt sphinxes were usually male, but in ancient Greece sphinxes had wings and were female.

4. Egyptian men and women wore clothes made of linen. Do you know which plant is grown to make linen?

Linen is made from the flax plant. This useful plant also provides linseed oil.

8. THE PRINCE, THE DOG, THE SNAKE AND THE CROCODILE

1. *Why did the king of Egypt make his son live all alone in the house in the desert?*

The king made his son live all alone in the house in the desert because he thought that this would protect him from his three fates.

2. *What were the three fates that threatened the prince?*

The prince was threatened by the dog, the snake and the crocodile.

3. *Why did the princes spend all their time jumping in front of the princess's tower?*

They were jumping to reach the window in the high tower. The prince who reached the window first would be able to marry the beautiful princess.

4. *I have written my own ending to the story. Can you write one?*

This is up to you - there is no right answer to this question!

9. THE STORY OF TRUTH AND FALSEHOOD

1. Can you remember how Falsehood described his lost dagger?

Falsehood said that his dagger was huge, as big as a mountain. It had a massive copper blade as long as the River Nile and an enormous carved handle made from one hundred trees. It was also incredibly expensive.

2. What did the boy give to the herdsman?

The boy gave the herdsman ten loaves of bread, a walking stick, a pair of sandals, a jug of water and a sword.

3. Did the boy really have a massive ox?

No. He did have a beautiful ox but it was not as big as he said it was! No ox could really be as large as the land of Egypt.

4. Why did Falsehood think that Truth was dead?

Falsehood thought that Truth was dead because his servants had told him that they had seen him being eaten by a lion in the desert.

10. THE BATTLE OF KADESH

1. Why did Ramesses think that the enemy were camped a long way from Kadesh?

Ramesses believed the first two secret agents who told him that the enemy was camped a long way from Kadesh.

2. How did he realise that they were hiding nearby?

The Egyptian soldiers captured two more secret agents, and these two told Ramesses the truth.

3. Which god helped Ramesses when he was fighting all alone?

Ramesses was helped by Amen, the warrior god of Thebes.

4. Why do you think Ramesses exaggerates his part in the battle?

Ramesses exaggerates his part in the battle so that everyone who reads the story (including you) will think that he is the bravest man in the world.